G. P. PUTNAM'S SONS
An imprint of Penguin Random House LLC, New York

First published in the United States of America by G. P. Putnam's Sons,
an imprint of Penguin Random House LLC, 2022
Text copyright © 2022 by Gibson Frazier
Illustrations copyright © 2022 by Micah Player
G. P. Putnam's Sons is a registered trademark of Penguin Random House LLC.

Visit us online at penguinrandomhouse.com

Library of Congress Cataloging-in-Publication Data is available.

Manufactured in China
ISBN 9780525517146

1 3 5 7 9 10 8 6 4 2

TOPL

Design by Marikka Tamura
Text set in Superclarendon
The drawings in this book were made by hand on
a Surface Studio 2 in Adobe Photoshop and Fresco.

To the one and only Dash: I love ya, kid.
—G.F.

To all the little kids with BIG feelings.
—M.P.

Dash Gordon dragged his feet on the sidewalk all the way home from karate class. He was in a gloomy mood. It had not been a good morning.

Dash loved karate.

He loved it so much that sometimes he forgot
Sensei's number one rule: No talking in class.

He always wanted to be good, but sometimes Dash's feelings controlled him, instead of the other way around.

SHHHH

As Dash and his father walked up to their apartment, Dash froze at the top of the stairs. The sweetest aroma had crept into the hallway. It shocked Dash's nostrils, breakdanced on the back of his throat, and plunged down to his lungs.

The ambrosial scent of oatmeal walnut chocolate chip cookies could only mean one thing: "GRANDMA NONI!"

Dash's chest
felt warm and fuzzy.
His toes danced.

His fingers tickled the air.

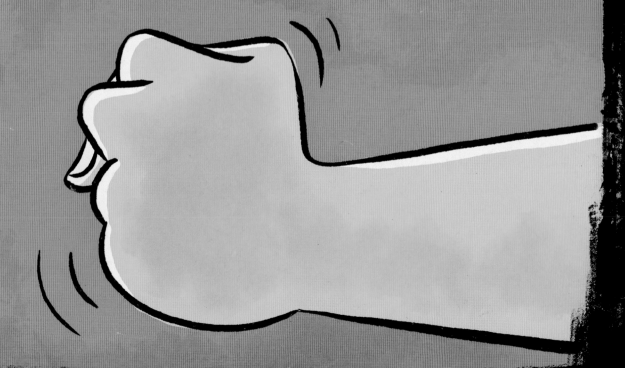

His hands clenched into the position
Dash called the Dragon's Fist.

Dash leapt through the open door,
and before he knew what was happening,
the Dragon's Fist came down on Noni's tray.
Cookies flew everywhere.

Grandma Noni shook her head.

Tears rolled down
Dash's face.
His day had gone
from bad to worse.

That afternoon, Dash went to Cate Shanahan's
birthday party.

It was a gymnastics party, and all of Cate's guests
raced through an obstacle course that ended with a zip line
into a pit of foam balls.

HAPPY BIRTH

DAY, CATE!

Dash was in heaven.

When it was time to eat, Mrs. Shanahan made
Dash sit right next to her so she could keep
an eye on him. After all, she didn't want
a repeat of what happened LAST year.

Suddenly, the lights went out, and Mrs. Shanahan put a big,
round cake down in front of Cate. The flickering light of six
white candles (plus one to grow on) illuminated Cate's face, and
all the kids whooped and cheered as they sang "Happy Birthday."

Dash imagined his *own* birthday party. He pictured the cake that *he* would have. He imagined the candles on *his* cake. He thought about the wish that *he* would make—a brand-new bicycle.

Dash's chest felt warm and fuzzy.
His toes danced.
His fingers tickled the air.

Dash blew out the candles on his cake.

WHOOSH!

The room went silent. Dash looked around to discover that he had actually blown out all of Cate's birthday candles.

Cate glared at Dash.
Mrs. Shanahan shook her head.
Tears rolled down Dash's face.

The day wasn't getting any better.

The next morning at school, Dash was determined to be on his best behavior.

Ms. Chang gathered the class on the rug and guided them through counting number squares.

Dash loved counting the red dots that filled the black squares. And he could even get to one hundred if he counted them in groups of ten.

But Sienna was having a harder time with it.

As Sienna counted each red dot, Dash's chest started to feel warm and fuzzy.

Sienna stared at the squares. Dash's toes danced. His fingers tickled the air.

Before he knew what was happening, Dash jumped
to his feet, and the numbers poured out of his mouth.

All of Dash's friends glared at him. Ms. Chang shook her head.

Tears rolled down Sienna's face.

"Sorry, Sienna," Dash said, sniffling.

This was the worst of all possible days.

That night, Dash's mother read him a story from his favorite book, *The Adventures of Robin Hood.* But Dash wasn't paying attention. All he could think about was Sienna, and Cate, and Grandma Noni.

"What's the matter, sweetie?" his mom asked.

Dash sighed. "I karate-chopped Noni's cookies. I ruined Cate's birthday wish. I didn't let Sienna count her numbers. I know what's right and wrong, but sometimes I just can't help myself. Why are my feelings so much bigger than me?"

"It's been a rough couple of days,"
his mom said, pulling Dash in for
a hug. "But I have an idea.
Sit up and close your eyes."

He did.
His mom continued, "First,
let's smell Noni's cookies."

Dash pictured Grandma Noni holding a plate of her delicious cookies as he took a deep breath in.

"Next, let's blow out Cate's candles."

Dash imagined the glowing candles on top of Cate's cake and pushed all the air from his lungs.

"Now let's count Sienna's numbers."

Dash whispered, "Ten, twenty, thirty, forty, fifty, sixty, seventy, eighty, ninety, one hundred."

"How do you feel now?" his mom asked.

Dash opened his eyes. His chest felt calm and cool.
His toes were still. His hands relaxed.

Surprised, Dash said, "I feel good."

"Good or great?"

"Great!" he announced with a smile.

Dash went to sleep that night excited for school in the morning.

The next afternoon, during choice time, Dash and his friends were hard at work making perfect paper airplanes.

Dash's plane was so sleek and beautiful, he knew he could send it soaring so that it landed in the trash can all the way across the room.

But Ms. Chang had many rules, and one of them was

NO THROWING PAPER AIRPLANES DURING CHOICE TIME

Dash wanted to throw the plane.
He NEEDED to throw the plane, but he knew that he shouldn't.
Dash's chest felt warm and fuzzy.
His toes danced. His fingers tickled the air.

Then, Dash remembered
his plan.
He closed his eyes.

He smelled the cookies.

He blew out the candles.

He counted to one hundred.

And all of a sudden, Dash's feelings
didn't seem so big anymore.
He smiled. Dash opened his eyes,
placed the airplane in his backpack,
and returned to his seat.

Dash's father picked him up after school,
and they walked together to the park.

When they got to their favorite spot,
Dash grabbed the paper airplane from
his backpack and climbed up onto a rock.